TONY HAWK'S 900 revolution

VOLUME 13

Tony Hawk's 900 Revolution
is published by Stone Arch Books, a Capstone imprint,
1710 Roe Crest Drive, North Mankato, MN 56003
www.capstonepub.com

Cataloging-in-Publication Data is available on the Library
of Congress website.
ISBN: 978-1-4342-6032-1 (library binding)
ISBN: 978-1-4342-6218-9 (paperback)

Summary: In this final book of the series, the surviving
members of the Revolution reunite under the leadership of
Zeke Grebes, Omar's long lost father. They're badly beaten,
but together this NEW REVOLUTION team hopes to win back
their stolen Fragments. However, the final pieces won't
come easily. Only an epic, skate-or-die battle will reunite
the pieces and bring Tony Hawk's 900 skateboard—and its
power—back together again.

Photo and Vector Graphics Credits: Shutterstock
Photo credit page 122, Bart Jones/ Tony Hawk

Cover Illustrator: Benny Fuentes
Graphic Designer: Kay Fraser and Hilary Wacholz

Printed in China.
032013
007228RRDF13

HORIZON

BY BRANDON TERRELL // ILLUSTRATED BY WILSON TORTOSA

VOLUME 13

STONE ARCH BOOKS
a capstone imprint

ON JULY 27, 1999 . . .

TONY HAWK LANDED THE FIRST-EVER 900.

SKATEBOARD

ERGY COLLECTION

OWER DESTIN

LYPSE HORIZO

ECTION FRAGMENT

OWER REVOLUTIO

ORIZON QUEST

VOLUTION HAWK

1

Elliot Addison sat in the backseat of a black SUV, staring out his window at Paris. He had traveled the world more than he ever thought possible. He'd seen sights that would leave other teens envious. All of these experiences were on behalf of the Collective, an organization dedicated to recovering the pieces of a mystical skateboard with unlimited power.

Elliot could feel the end of the mission approaching. The Collective had nearly every Fragment of Tony Hawk's 900 skateboard in their possession. Their competition, the Revolution, was adrift and leaderless. And Elliot's mentor, an unnerving man named Archard Venin, was taking him to see the Collective's creator, the Old Man.

The SUV drove out of the city and into the French countryside. Elliot shifted in his seat. *I always believed the Old Man was a myth used to strike fear in the Collective and to rally them behind a common cause,* he thought.

Archard Venin sat beside Elliot, calmly reading a French newspaper. A leather attaché case rested between them. "This visit is nothing to worry about," Venin told him, not looking up from his paper.

"Excuse me?" asked Elliot.

"You're nervous." Venin folded the paper before finally glancing at Elliot with his dark, piercing eyes.

"I'm sorry, Mr. Venin," Elliot said.

"Nothing to apologize for. But you need not worry. Now should be a time to celebrate, right?" A thin smile spread across Venin's lips.

Elliot nodded. "Absolutely." But, in truth, he didn't feel like celebrating. He knew the Collective's mission in San Diego had been a failure. The Revolution had somehow obtained not only more of the Fragments but also a girl who Lora claimed actually was a Fragment.

The SUV ascended a winding driveway lined with hundreds of trees. At the end of the drive was an enormous mansion made of brick and stone. Ivy covered much of the walls.

The SUV stopped. Elliot grabbed the leather case, and the two men exited. Venin buttoned his suit coat and led the way into the home. Elliot followed at his heels, clutching tightly to the attaché case.

The mansion's foyer was a majestic room dimly lit by a crystal chandelier. Flanking the far end of the room was a winding double staircase. Venin walked briskly up the steps. Elliot took the stairs two at a time to keep pace. They walked down a long hall. At the end, two guards were positioned near a thick, oak door.

"Bonjour, monsieur," said the first guard, a wiry man with a thin beard.

"Bonjour." The second guard, a burly man, opened the door for them.

The room was dark, and it took Elliot's eyes a moment to adjust. It was a bedroom. A large armoire and dresser sat against one wall. Atop the dresser sat a small television— its volume turned low—tuned to a French news station. The blinds were drawn, blocking out all but a sliver of daylight.

The room smelled like a hospital. Elliot wrinkled his nose. Rhythmic beeping came from several machines surrounding the bed; their numbers glowed green and red in the dark.

Lying in the bed, perched upon a pile of pillows, with tubes snaking around him, was the Old Man. He looked frail, like bones wrapped in tissue paper. His skin was translucent. He stared at Elliot.

Elliot nodded his head and looked away. The Old Man's penetrating eyes made his skin crawl.

Venin poured a glass of water from a pitcher beside the bed. He offered it to the Old Man. *"Peré,"* he said quietly. Elliot didn't know much French, but he knew the word for "father."

Wait. The Old Man is Mr. Venin's dad?

"Grebes and Otus are out of our way." Venin talked like a child trying to impress a parent.

The Old Man took a long drink of water and spoke. His voice was weak, like cracking ice. "Your old friends," he said. "You did this...for me?"

"I will do whatever it takes to complete the 900 board for you. Whatever I must do to save you from this..." Venin waved a hand at the medical equipment. "...life. To give you strength again. Power. I have something for you, *Peré.*"

He nodded at Elliot, who went to the bedside and offered Venin the leather case. Venin took it, unclasped it, and presented the Old Man with its contents.

A large splinter of wood, old and brittle, lay nestled in foam packing. It was clearly not from the 900 board, but the Old Man's eyes lit up at the sight of it.

"David Solomon recovered it from the ashes of the San Francisco fire," Venin said. "*Peré*, we have tracked the final Fragment. Soon, we will possess them all, save the handful still controlled by the Revolution teens."

The Old Man took the wooden shard from the case and ran it through his gnarled fingers. "You have—" He broke into a fit of coughs. When he had regained his composure, he wiped his mouth with a white handkerchief and finished. "—done well."

"Thank you, *Peré.* I have sent Tommy Goff to recover the final Fragment. He will not fail." Venin leaned over, placed a kiss upon the Old Man's forehead, and said, "Rest now."

"Yes," the Old Man said, closing his eyes and grasping the wooden splinter to his chest.

Venin crossed the room and, without a word, he and Elliot exited. Elliot's nerves had not been settled; in fact, the more he knew, the more anxious he became.

With a final look at the bedroom door, behind which the Old Man clung to life, Elliot Addison followed his mentor down the hall.

2

"All right, class, follow me." Ms. Nussbaum's voice echoed off the walls of the museum. Fifteen-year-old Autumn Rose, who was admiring the towering skeleton of a *Tyrannosaurus rex*, hurried over to rejoin her class. They shuffled along toward the next exhibit.

Autumn clearly stood out among her peers. She wore a bright yellow dress, a pair of jeans, and matching yellow skate shoes. Her long, wavy, red hair cascaded around her neck and shoulders.

It was late morning, and Autumn's school was visiting the Smithsonian's National Museum of Natural History on a field trip. It was her first time at the museum, and she was in love with the place.

Autumn found her best friends, Chelsea and Hazel, at the back of the pack. "Hey," she said. "This place is insane. So cool!"

Chelsea rolled her eyes. "Only you, Autumn."

"What do you mean?" she asked.

Hazel counted off with her fingers. "Cheerleader. Athlete. And a big old nerd."

Autumn clapped her hands and made up a cheer. "Hey, hey, what can I say? I'm all kinds of awesome, and you're just a-okay!"

The trio of girls laughed, and Chelsea playfully slugged Autumn on the shoulder. Then they followed the rest of the class through the first floor's rotunda and into a wide-open space called Ocean Hall.

The exhibit was breathtaking. Models of marine life adorned the walls and hung from the ceiling. Autumn wandered through the hall, taking it all in.

At the far end of the hall was a darkened alcove. It was meant for special exhibits but was closed. A sign on a metal stand read: Coming Soon, Life in Pompeii.

Autumn heard a noise inside the closed exhibit. She ducked under the velvet rope blocking off the alcove. Inside the exhibit, an older teenage boy was hunched over a podium filled with artifacts.

"You're not supposed to be back here," Autumn said.

The boy jumped at the sound of her voice. He turned to face her. Even in the dark, she could see he was cute. His bleach-blond hair hung in his face.

"Sorry," the boy said. "I must have gotten turned around in this huge place."

"Uh-huh." Autumn wasn't buying it. The guy looked guilty of something.

"Just leave me alone," he muttered, lowering his head and walking toward her. Autumn saw his fist was clenched at his side. She looked up at the podium. Then back at the boy.

"Wait," she said, stopping him. "Let me see your hand."

"What?" He tried to look innocent.

"You took something, didn't you?" she said.

Autumn reached out, grabbed him by the wrist, and pried open his closed fist. Sure enough, the boy held a small sliver of wood. It looked worthless, not like something you'd steal from a museum.

Autumn plucked it from his hand. "I should totally call security."

"Just…give it back to me," said the boy.

"No. It's not yours. It's—" Autumn began.

Fwoom!

Suddenly, the wood splinter in her hand erupted in a burst of blue light. Autumn yelped as bolts of electricity coursed along her fingers and wrist.

"What is this thing?" she whispered.

The boy advanced on her. "You're a Key," he said.

"A what?"

Autumn backed up until she was in the Ocean Hall again. She looked frantically about, trying to find a security guard or her teacher or anyone. Her class had disappeared, though, leaving the hall mostly vacant except for a few tourists, three men in black suits, and a couple of teenagers wearing black hoodies and jeans. In their hands were skateboards.

The piece of wood in her palm twitched. The mysterious fragment stretched and grew until Autumn was holding a sleek, glowing skateboard.

"Hand it over," the boy said.

Autumn was in danger. Every instinct told her she needed to get away from the teen.

Well, why not put this thing to good use?

Autumn dropped the board and, with lightning-quick speed, pushed off, skating across Ocean Hall at top speed.

"Stop!" Autumn looked back and saw the men in black running after her. The teens dropped their boards and pushed off.

Autumn was a natural skateboarder. She'd been riding all her life and was fearless on a deck. The skateboard beneath her feet crackled with energy. It moved with a power all its own, gliding effortlessly along the museum floor. She curved around startled tourists, searching for an exit. There, in the rotunda, was a large set of stairs. She pushed with her back foot, bent low, and aimed for it.

The stairs were thankfully empty, and when Autumn reached them, she ollied into the air and hit the rail right between her trucks in a flawless Smith grind. She landed softly at the bottom of the first set of stairs, where they turned and continued toward ground level.

Wow! A girl could get used to this, she thought.

Something whizzed past her shoulder and struck the wall with a crack. She looked back and saw one of the men holding some kind of dart gun pointed at her. Autumn ducked, leaped off the board, kicked it into her hands, and bounded down the remainder of the steps.

She sprinted through the museum's ground floor, past a bustling café, and toward the museum exit.

One of the glass doors was open. Autumn jumped onto the azure deck and pushed with all her strength.

Autumn burst through the open door and out of the museum. A wide set of stairs led to the street. The frightened teen ollied into the air, grabbed the nose of her board, and kicked out her feet in a perfect airwalk. Landing on the sidewalk, she glanced back at the museum's entrance.

The teenagers were still on her tail.

She looked left and right, spotted the towering monolithic Washington Monument, and pushed off down the sidewalk, heading along Constitution Avenue toward the populated National Mall.

She coasted along, weaving around pedestrians. At one point, she was forced to swerve into the street, kickflipping off the curb. She saw Constitution Gardens and the Reflecting Pool to her left. It was a beautiful morning, and the sites were swarming with people.

She was beginning to think she'd lost her pursuers in the crowd when a black SUV roared up behind her. She craned her neck and saw the teen from the museum sitting in the passenger seat. Panic raced through her veins. The blue energy seemed to pick up on her anxiety, and a shot of adrenaline rushed through her.

The teen leaned out his window, aiming a dart gun at her. Autumn looked for something to hide behind but found nothing.

A stylish motorcycle roared in from her left, blocking the teen's aim. The bike was miraculously protecting her. The SUV accelerated, trying to shove the motorcycle off the road. The bike swerved to avoid a collision.

They raced down the middle of the street. Autumn tried to calm herself, but her breath hitched in her throat. She curved left, performed a combination ollie and wild ride over a patch of grass, and landed on the sidewalk at the base of the Lincoln Memorial. She lost her focus and nearly struck a man with a humongous camera snapping a photo. As she corrected herself, her foot slipped from her deck, and she was forced to bail.

Instinct kicked in, and as she fell toward the cement, Autumn threw her hands in front of her. Pebbles and stones bit into her palms, and she could feel the road rash on her arms. She struggled to pull herself up.

The motorcycle screeched to a stop. Its rider leaped off, wrenching the helmet from his head. He was in his twenties, with dark hair and a serious demeanor. He ran toward Autumn.

Autumn looked for her board, but she couldn't find it. Instead, lying nearby was the splinter of wood; the glowing deck had transformed back into a useless artifact.

The teens chasing her on skateboards had arrived. As the motorcyclist approached, the first skater blew past him, striking him in the shin with a baton. The man cried out in anguish, but he remained on his feet. A second raced by, but this time the man was prepared. He ducked as the teen swung at him.

The SUV came to a stop mere feet from Autumn. She saw the passenger door open and the blond teen leap out. He strode across the cement toward her.

"Help!" Autumn screamed. The teen seized the wooden splinter off the ground. It burned crimson in his hand.

The motorcyclist caught the teen from behind, grabbing him at the waist and tackling him to the ground. They grappled with one another, trading blows until the teen pointed the wooden splinter at the man and blasted him with a jolt of red electricity. He slumped over, defeated.

The teenager teetered to his feet. He laughed. "Things are never easy with you, are they, Rafe?"

The motorcyclist coughed and spit blood onto the pavement but said nothing.

Motioning to the surrounding skaters, the teen said, "Bring the Key. Venin will want to use her as leverage." He noticed a crowd beginning to gather around them and clapped his hand. "Quick. Before the cops show up."

Autumn's heart raced. *They're talking about me.* She scrambled to her feet, tried to run, but was surrounded. One of the skaters, a kid with a buzz cut, grabbed her and lifted her off her feet. Autumn kicked and squirmed, but it didn't help. He clamped a hand over her mouth before she could scream.

She was whisked to the waiting SUV, which peeled off as sirens sliced through the quiet morning air.

NERGY
OWER DESTIN
LYPSE HORIZO
ECTION FRAGMENT
WER REVOLUTIO
ORIZON QUEST
OLUTION HAW

3

Omar couldn't stop staring.

It was midafternoon, and he was sitting in a booth at a hole-in-the-wall Mexican diner, looking out the window at the parking lot. There, pacing alongside a gray passenger van, was his dad, Zeke Grebes.

Until last night, Omar believed his father was dead. Then Zeke had appeared at their abandoned home in San Diego—where the Revolution teens were hiding out—and Omar's world had been tipped upside down.

Since then, Omar hadn't slept a wink. He didn't want to take his eyes off his father for fear that, if he looked away, Zeke would disappear like a ghost.

The team had been on the road since before sunrise. It was now past lunchtime, and they had stopped to refuel both the van and themselves.

The restaurant was in a small Arizona town a couple of miles off the freeway. In fact, they were only about an hour from the Revolution's old training facility outside of Phoenix.

Man, it feels like an eternity since we stayed at that place, thought Omar.

Seated in the booth next to him was Neelu Otus, a knockout beauty with caramel-colored dreadlocks. Across from them sat Joey Rail, a jokester who rocked on a BMX, and the Revolution's newest and most unique member, a girl named Fiona Skylark.

"Any idea where we're going?" Joey asked, shoveling a tortilla loaded with guacamole into his mouth.

Omar shook his head. "No clue." Though he did have an inkling.

Fiona lifted her water glass to eye level. Blue energy coursed through her fingers and electrified the glass. The water inside bubbled and fizzed. "I can't believe I never knew I could do this."

Joey forced her arm down. "Yo, Little Miss Fragment, keep it on the DL. We don't want to spook the locals." He glanced around at the diner's half-dozen patrons. None were looking in their direction; all of them appeared beyond bored.

Fiona smiled. "Wait. Isn't one of your mottos, 'Flaunt it if you've got it'?"

"Well sure, but by *it* I mean your sweet, uh, skateboarding skills, not the mystical artifact wedged against your spine." He winked. Fiona rolled her eyes.

Outside, Zeke snapped the cell phone shut and ran his hands over his bearded face in exhaustion. *Something isn't right*, Omar surmised.

"How are you holding up, Omar?" Neelu's voice was soft in his ear. His heart fluttered briefly.

Omar shrugged. "It's…surreal. I thought I'd never see him again. This is like a miracle, you know?" He immediately regretted his word choice. "I'm so sorry," he quickly added.

Neelu's father, Eldrick Otus, had been the team's mentor. He and many of the Revolution elders had recently been killed in a bomb blast orchestrated by a Collective agent named David Solomon. Neelu had seen the explosion and was still numb with shock.

"Your dad's waving for us, O," Joey said through a mouthful of burrito.

The gang dropped enough cash on the table to pay the bill, then exited the diner. The dry Arizona heat took Omar's breath away.

Zeke Grebes did a quick head count. "Where are the others?"

"Over here!" said Slider. He and Amy rode their skateboards across the asphalt. In Amy's hand was a large plastic bag from a nearby gas station. As they crossed, Slider popped up and performed a Smith grind across a length of curb.

When she reached them, Amy ground her board to a stop. "Got us some road snacks," she said. "And some new duds. The pickings were slim."

"Let me guess. Slider found himself a nice new Diamondbacks cap," Joey said.

"You wish. I bleed blue, baby." Slider, a born and bred New Yorker, adjusted the bill of his Yankees cap.

"Come on," Zeke said, visibly upset. "Load up."

The gang clambered into the van. Before joining them, Omar asked, "Is everything okay, Dad?" *Wow, it feels weird to say that.*

Zeke placed a large hand on Omar's shoulder. "I know I owe you an explanation," he said. "When we get where we're going, this will all make sense."

"Okay." Even though he hadn't seen his father in years, Omar trusted the man completely. It was a good feeling to have again.

Zeke cupped his hand on the back of Omar's neck. "I missed you, kiddo."

Omar's eyes started watering. He fisted away the tears and said, "Right back at ya."

Then Omar took shotgun, and the team resumed their drive.

***

By the time the Revolution neared their destination, the sun was low in the west, and the sky was a breathtaking mixture of oranges and reds. Their snack supply had been depleted, and they had passed from Arizona into the flat, desert-like plateaus of New Mexico. Amy and Slider lay in the far back, legs tangled together, napping. Fiona and Joey were speaking to each other in low voices while each sported one earbud from a pair attached to an MP3 player. It didn't take a rocket scientist to see that Joey had feelings for the girl. Omar looked into the side mirror at Neelu. She was seated directly behind him, her nose buried in an electronic notepad. She hadn't said a word in hours.

The van slowed as it passed a wooden sign beside the road. On the sign was the painted image of a gray alien standing beside a flying saucer. Below it read: Make First Contact in Roswell! 10 miles ahead!

"Gnarly," Joey said. "Please tell me we're heading to Area 51 and that the Revolution is tracking UFOs now."

Zeke didn't answer. He simply eyed Joey up in the rearview mirror. Then he hung a left onto a narrow, two-lane road, turned to Omar, and said, "Is he always like that?"

Omar shrugged. "Pretty much."

A mile up the road, the van turned onto a hidden gravel path. Rising against the flat earth in the distance was a forgotten, ramshackle shed made of corrugated metal and wood. Behind it was a large warehouse. They were the only buildings on the horizon. Zeke pulled the van up beside the shed, and the gang staggered out, stretching their arms and legs. Then Zeke removed a large duffel bag containing the Fragments and a few other supplies from the rear of the van.

"Where are we?" Fiona asked.

Omar saw the side of the shed and knew the answer.

There, stenciled on the metal wall with green spray paint, was a graffiti tag. A triangular image of a diving bird, wings tucked at its side, beak open.

"The Wyvern," Omar answered.

"Ain't she a beaut?" Zeke said with a smile, leading the way into the shed.

It was vacant. Empty. Just a locked metal box positioned waist-high on the wall. Zeke drew a thin chain from around his neck. Attached to it was a small key. He inserted the key into the lock, and the box popped open. Inside was an ominous red button.

"You may want to hold on to something," he said. Then he pressed the button.

The floor groaned, and the whole thing began to sink into the ground. It caught Omar off guard. He spread his legs to distribute his weight. He saw the others doing the same. Joey dropped to one knee.

"What's going on?" Slider asked.

"Relax," Zeke answered simply.

The creaking floor was a giant, secret elevator. After a long, slow descent, the floor shuddered and stopped. A large metal door stood before them. It opened, revealing a white room lit with florescent bulbs.

Omar was too awestruck to move a muscle.

The room contained a bank of computer hard drives, two rows of monitors, and a wall filled with an array of flat-screen televisions. Many of the monitors featured maps; others seemed to be tracking a person or object. A few played news broadcasts or footage from various action sports competitions.

About ten men and women, along with a handful of teenagers, sat at the computers.

The team stepped from the elevator as a single, dumbfounded unit.

A teenage boy, tall with thick-rimmed glasses and curly black hair, approached. He was dressed in a David Bowie graphic T-shirt, jeans, and a pair of skate shoes, and he looked like he knew his way around a half-pipe.

"Welcome back, Mr. Grebes," the teen said. "We've established communication with Rafe. He's in Paris."

"Good," Zeke replied. "Give me one moment."

"Did you say Rafe?" Omar asked. Warren Rafe had been one of the Revolution team's mentors. He'd disappeared shortly before Eldrick and the other Elders had lost their lives in San Francisco.

"Yes," Zeke said. Upon seeing the looks of disbelief on the team's faces, he added, "Kids, I know this is a lot to take in. With everything that's happened to all of you over the last few months, I'm surprised you're even still standing."

"Wait a sec," Slider said. Anger flushed red in his cheeks. "I don't get it. While we've been out there risking our tails, you've all just been hiding out down here?"

Zeke shook his head. "It's not that simple. The Wyvern was built as a fail-safe set to activate only in the event that either the Elders were killed or that the Collective neared completion of the 900 board."

"Both of which have happened," Fiona said quietly.

"Did my father know about the Wyvern?" Neelu asked.

Zeke responded honestly with a simple nod.

"They're going to do it, aren't they?" There was grave concern in Amy's voice. "The Collective is going to complete the 900 board, and…and this is what? The Revolution's fallout shelter?"

Zeke considered her question before answering. "Yes. I suppose so."

"And what happens if they get the final pieces?" Joey asked. "What if they get a hold of our Fragments?"

"Honestly, we don't know," said Zeke.

"I do," Omar said. He remembered the lifelike vision he'd had of a post-apocalyptic world, one where the Revolution had been defeated, where his friends were either dead or disbanded, and where— "The adults become zombies."

"Huh?" Joey said. "Zombies? Like George Romero, 'I wanna eat your brains' zombies?"

Omar shook his head. "No. But anyone over twenty, it was like...like their minds were just wiped. The Collective didn't have the entire deck yet, but they had enough to make a mess of the whole world."

"Was this another one of your visions?" Neelu quietly asked.

"Yeah."

Zeke pondered this a moment, then turned to the teen with the glasses and said, "Get the Architect down here. And patch me through to Warren."

"On it." The boy rushed over to his computer and donned a set of headphones as Zeke approached the wall of monitors. On one of the screens, a female reporter stood in front of a domed building lined with columns. The banner at the bottom of the screen read, Theft and Altercation at Smithsonian Confounds Police.

A door at the far end of the room burst open, and a disheveled man stepped inside. He carried in his hands a computer tablet, quickly punching buttons. He looked oddly familiar to Omar.

He must be the Architect.

The Architect walked over to Zeke, and the two spoke in low voices. Then Zeke motioned to Omar. "Join us," he said.

Omar walked around the bank of computers and stood at his father's side. He stared at the Architect, still trying to puzzle out where he'd seen the dude with the tired, bloodshot eyes and deep crow's feet before.

"Hello, Omar," the Architect said.

Zeke placed a hand on Omar's shoulder and said, "Son, I know it's been a while, but do you remember Henry Goff?"

Omar's stomach dropped like he'd just done a backside heel flip off a monster gap. He stared in disbelief at the Architect, trying to formulate words. Finally, he managed to say, "Tommy's dad?"

Henry Goff had abandoned his family when Tommy was just a kid, and the fallout had been devastating. The Grebes had taken Tommy in like a second son. To see the man who had ruined Tommy's life here, now, as a part of the Revolution, it was almost too much to take.

"How could you just leave them?" Omar asked, anger building inside of him now. "You ruined your whole family."

"Omar—" Zeke began.

"No! And you...you knew?" Omar shrugged his father's hand from his shoulder. "Is that why you made Tommy a part of our family? Because you felt guilty?"

"I promised Henry I'd watch over him," Zeke said.

"I left my family for the Revolution," Henry Goff said. There was sadness in his voice. "And it has broken my heart every day since. But I was instructed to build the Wyvern. It was my duty, and I did it willingly. That doesn't mean I don't have regrets."

"Regrets?" Omar was furious. "Your son is a member of the Collective now!"

"His head has been filled with lies and deceit," Zeke said. "Because of Archard Venin, Tommy believes his destiny is to save the world."

"But he's going to destroy it," Omar said.

Henry Goff's shoulders fell. "You can still save him, Omar," he said. "Please save him."

Omar didn't know how to respond to that.

The largest screen in the center of the wall suddenly went black. When it blinked back to life, Omar was looking at a pixilated image of Warren Rafe.

"Zeke, it looks like you have company," Rafe said. His voice was digitized, breaking in and out. "Good to see you kids safe."

"What's your status, Rafe?" Zeke asked.

"I've followed the Collective from Washington, D.C., to a location a few clicks outside of Paris," Rafe replied.

Henry Goff tapped a few buttons on his notepad, and the surrounding monitors on the wall now displayed a terrain map of France. The image zoomed in until Omar could see the streets of Paris and the winding Seine River cutting through it. A red blip appeared southwest of the city.

"They seem to have brought both the girl and the Fragment to a well protected villa. The rest of the Fragments must be inside, too. We're running out of time, Zeke."

"Any sign of Venin?" Zeke asked.

"Affirmative. Tommy as well."

"And the girl? You believe she's another Key?"

"Affirmative," Henry replied.

"Okay. Continue surveillance, and we'll have backup in the air ASAP."

"Copy that." The monitor went black again.

Silence hung heavily in the room.

Finally, Zeke turned to face the Revolution team, who remained rooted to their spots near the elevator. He opened his mouth to speak, but Joey beat him to it.

"Let me guess," Joey said. "We're off to Paris?"

"*Oui*," answered Zeke.

4

Less than two hours after arriving at the Wyvern, the Revolution team was heading out once more. Omar was placed in charge of the remaining Fragments. The handful of artifacts were secured in a lead-lined box, then placed in his backpack for safekeeping.

Omar was overly tired, but he knew the power stored inside the small, composite wheel Fragment in his pocket would keep him from complete exhaustion. With all of the traveling the Revolution did, this was a huge relief.

Zeke led the team outside. Darkness had settled over the open stretch of desert; the expansive sky glittered with stars. The team walked from the shed to the warehouse, where Zeke opened a large metal door.

Inside the warehouse was a training facility, complete with a thirty-foot pipe, mini-ramps, a handful of fun boxes, and numerous rails and ledges. A Blackhawk helicopter sat at the far side of the training area, with a very familiar barrel-chested man leaning against its hull.

"Sam!" Omar's voice echoed through the warehouse. Sam Forrest was the Revolution's pilot. He had not been seen since he'd flown Eldrick and Neelu to San Francisco. Omar had assumed he'd perished in the blast.

"Hey, guys." Sam lifted his right arm to wave, and Omar noticed that it was tightly wrapped with white bandages. As they got closer, he also saw burn marks along the pilot's neck and cheek.

"Are you okay?" Omar asked.

Sam nodded. "I'll be fine. Just lucky to be here." He looked at Neelu. "I'm real sorry, little lady."

She said nothing but gave him a quick hug.

As the team began to load into the helicopter, the warehouse ceiling retracted, yawning open with a rumble to reveal the starry sky.

Omar shook his head in wonder, then leaped aboard the helicopter as Sam flipped on the rotors and prepared to take off.

***

As the Blackhawk circled the airfield at Charles De Gaulle Airport in Paris, Omar checked his GPS watch, which he'd set to Central European Time. It was nearly dinnertime. No wonder his stomach seemed to be eating itself.

He'd dozed a bit on the flight, but not much. Every time he closed his eyes, he saw images from the past. The zombified adults from his crazy vision. Tommy standing atop the volcano in Hawaii. Eldrick the way he looked the first time Omar entered the Revolution Skate Shop an eternity and a half ago. *So much has happened, and it all feels like it's snowballing so fast I can't catch my breath.* The end was near, that much he knew. What he didn't know was how it was going to end, and it was this uncertainty that made Omar restless.

Zeke rented a battered black van from the airport, and the team rode south along the outskirts of the city, noshing on fast food bought at a restaurant in the terminal. *Nothing like coming to Paris and eating an airport hamburger,* Omar thought. But the greasy burger and watered-down soda actually hit the spot. And besides, there was no time to waste, especially not on fine cuisine.

Night had fallen, and the city was alive with lights. In the distance, Omar could see the twinkling outline of the Eiffel Tower. Maybe some day, when this was all over, he and Neelu would get a chance to explore the landmark. To act like a normal couple. That is, if the Collective didn't destroy the world before he had a chance to officially ask her to be his girlfriend.

They exited onto a narrow blacktop road, and Zeke killed the headlights, driving only by the soft glow of the moon. They crept along for another mile or so before coming to a stop.

"All right, everyone," Zeke said in a low voice. "Complete silence from here on out."

The teens quietly exited the van.

They walked along the dark road. The air was brisk, and Omar zipped up his black hoodie against the wind. The only sound was the scuff of their skate shoes along the pavement. As they approached a copse of trees, a silhouette appeared before them.

Warren Rafe.

Rafe spoke in low tones to Zeke, updating him on where the Collective was holding the girl—her name was Autumn—and how many security guards they had stationed around the mansion.

Without warning, a wave of nausea crashed into Omar and the horizon seemed to shift. He staggered forward as a tearing pain creased along his forehead.

"Vision," he whispered.

Next to him, Joey said, "What's that, O?"

"Going to have…"

And then—

He falls and twists and twirls in the wind before spreading his wings and letting the current catch him. It turns him up toward the night sky once more. He weaves his way through the metal beams and brilliant lights of the Eiffel Tower before angling off into darkness. Below him, first buildings and then fields pass by in a blur. He swoops low, passes over the heads of a cluster of people huddled in the road. He recognizes them, recognizes himself lying on his back. He does not stop but dives into the trees without pause, navigating the darkened maze of branches effortlessly. When he breaks free of the trees, he sees a sprawling home lit by floodlights. He alights on a windowsill high on the home's south wall. They are here. He cannot see them, but he knows this as fact. The Fragments are here. Here.

Omar awoke with a start. He was lying on the cool asphalt, his head resting on his backpack. His father knelt at his side.

"The Fragments are on the second floor," said Omar.

"Are you all right?" Zeke asked, running a calloused hand over Omar's forehead.

"Yeah, I'm good."

"Okay." Then, to the others, Zeke ordered, "Wait here." He removed a pair of night-vision binoculars from his pack, and he and Rafe disappeared into the thicket of trees.

An uncomfortable silence loomed over the group. Omar's stomach churned, and he cursed the airport food he'd downed earlier.

Five long minutes passed before Zeke and Rafe reemerged from the grove of trees. Both looked serious, determined. Zeke withdrew an electronic notebook from his pack. He crouched down in the middle of the road and placed the computer on the pavement.

"Gather around, everyone," he said. The teens did as directed. "Okay. Here's the plan."

***

After the plan was finalized, Zeke handed out earpieces to Neelu and Rafe. They wished one another good luck and separated into three groups. Rafe led Joey and Fiona west into the woods, where they were soon swallowed in shadow.

"Psst! Neelu," Omar whispered as she, Amy, and Slider walked off down the narrow cement road.

Neelu stopped and turned. "Yeah?"

"Good luck."

"You too. Be safe." She winked and rushed off to join the others.

That left Omar and his dad alone in the clearing.

"Are you sure you're okay?" Zeke asked.

Omar nodded.

"And you're positive the Fragments are on the second floor?"

"One hundred percent."

"All right, then. Let's go. And remember, kiddo—"

"Stay radical?" Omar interrupted.

Zeke winked. "Bingo."

Omar's heart swelled and, for the first time all night, he truly believed the Revolution had a chance of winning this battle.

He shouldered his pack and followed his dad into the thicket of trees. They walked for two hundred yards in the dark before the tree line ended in a brick wall.

Zeke threaded his fingers together and boosted Omar up and over. He landed gently at the underbrush. Zeke joined him a moment later.

From here, Omar could see the mansion. It was just as it had been in his vision. Floodlights around the perimeter of the home cast long, ominous shadows across the villa's stone and brick walls. Two teenage agents sat perched on the deck rail above the veranda. Their backs were to the yard, and they looked to be chatting. A spacious cement patio surrounded an empty, kidney-shaped pool. A third guard rode his skateboard along the patio. He casually flipped up his board, locked his trucks on the patio's metal rail in a feeble grind, landed, and rode along to the east side of the mansion.

When the coast was clear, Zeke motioned with one hand, and Omar followed him out across the open yard. If one of the guards on the veranda were to turn around, they'd be busted. But their luck held, and soon Omar and Zeke crouched in the veranda's shadows.

"We're in position," Zeke said into his earpiece.

***

Joey's team had made it to the property's west side, where they hid behind a four-stall garage adjacent to the mansion. An unguarded wooden door led into the house. Positioned high on the wall above the door was a black security camera. It oscillated back and forth, and Joey noticed a red light blinking on it.

Rafe drew them close and spoke low. "If I'm correct, this entrance leads to the formal dining room. We move after Neelu kills the feed to the security camera. Remember: get in, find the girl, and get out safe. Copy?"

"Got it." Joey drew the his father's parachute cord from his neck and wrapped it around his right hand. Fiona took his other hand and gave it a squeeze. He could feel the cool sizzle and pop of her energy pass through her fingers and wind its way around his arm. For a moment, her eyes glowed blue.

He watched the camera's blinking light and waited.

***

This could all end tonight.

The thought unnerved Amy. While she was ready for her life to no longer be in peril on a regular basis, she didn't dare think of what the world would be like if the Collective completed the 900 board. But what would happen if the Revolution won? Would she go back to Colorado, back to her old life of snowboarding powder-covered black diamond trails? *Could* she go back to her old life?

And what will happen with Dylan and me?

They were walking along a cement drive overhung by a canopy of trees.

According to Rafe, this would lead them directly to the guesthouse and utility shed nestled at the rear of the property. Amy walked beside Neelu, while Dylan rode his deck ahead of them, weaving back and forth, performing the occasional nose manual or power slide. A small crackle of blue energy trailed behind him.

Dylan reached the utility shed first and peered inside. "Coast is clear," he said.

Neelu tried the door, but it was locked. A keypad was positioned next to it.

"Here." Amy pulled the Fragment from her pocket, felt its charge course through her veins, and held it against the keypad. A single electric jolt struck the keypad, and Amy heard the lock disengage.

"Nice work," Dylan said, giving her a nudge.

The inside of the utility shed hummed. Neelu turned on her flashlight and searched the space. Along one wall was a set of three breaker boxes, the home's power supply. Along another, a network of wires led from a bank of hard drives into dual computer towers.

"There you are," Neelu said. She stepped to the computer and fired up the monitor. Neelu's fingers danced over the keyboard, completing the task in less than ten seconds.

Then she stood back and smugly said, "Open sesame," into her earpiece.

And she pressed *Enter*.

***

The camera above the door stopped moving, and its light winked out. Rafe led the others to the door. It was not locked, and the trio snuck in easily.

It was, in fact, a spacious dining room. In the dim moonlight cast through the windows, Joey saw a large crystal chandelier hanging over a long table in the middle of the room.

Of course, that wasn't all he saw.

"Guys," Joey said. "I found Autumn."

She was seated in a high-back chair, bound with heavy rope and wiggling against her restraints. A handkerchief was wrapped around her mouth. And at least two dozen Collective agents surrounded her.

A red light sparked in the middle of the room. Seated on the table, his legs dangling off the side and a Fragment held high in his hand, was Elliot Addison.

A broad grin spread across his face. "Come on in," he said. "We've been waiting for you."

And then the room glowed crimson with the light of two dozen Fragments.

***

Amy heard it first. The snap of a branch outside the utility shed's door. Someone was outside. Tendrils of Fragment electricity coursed along her arm as she turned to face the door.

There in the doorframe were three familiar figures. Peter—who went by the ridiculous nickname Buzzer—and his pals Rodney and Twitch.

"Hey, Kestrel," Peter said.

"Peter, what are you doing?" Amy asked. She and Peter had recently spent time stuck in the underground tomb of a forgotten Egyptian pharaoh. She'd hoped the experience had changed the teen's perspective. But alas, here he was, holding a crimson Fragment leveled at her.

"Yo. Ditch the Bluetooth," Rodney said to Neelu, scratching at the scar running the length of his face.

Neelu peeled off her earpiece and tossed it to Rodney, who caught it and flipped it over his shoulder. It landed in a patch of high grass.

"Now, let's have those Fragments of yours," Peter said with a wide smile.

***

It was so quiet Omar could hear Neelu's tiny voice in his father's earpiece. "Open sesame," she said.

Above them came the sound of a squawking radio, and the two teens guarding the veranda rushing off.

Zeke nodded. "That's our cue."

A wooden trellis was hidden beneath the thick ivy climbing the side of the house. Zeke reached into the greenery, grabbed the trellis, and began to shinny up.

Omar followed. As he reached the top, Zeke's hand clutched his hoodie and pulled him to safety. Two sliding glass doors led into the house.

"That one," Omar said, pointing at the right door.

The room they entered was a large study. Giant shelves crammed with books of all sizes lined the walls. A wooden ladder leaned against one of the shelves. An oak desk sat in the middle of the room.

And sitting behind the desk was Archard Venin.

"Ezekiel Grebes," Venin said calmly. "Good to see you again, old friend. You've brought Omar with you."

Without warning, Zeke jerked about spastically. Omar leaped back in shock and confusion. "Dad!"

Zeke's eyes rolled up in his head, and he slumped unconscious to the study's wooden floor. Behind him stood Tommy Goff and a black-haired girl named Lora. In Tommy's hand was a taser baton.

"Weird," Tommy said. "I thought I killed him already."

SKATEBOAR
NERGY COLLECTIO
OWER DESTIN
LYPSE HORIZO
ECTION FRAGMENT
WER REVOLUTIO
ORIZON QUEST
OLUTION HAW

5

"Don't get any ideas, Rail."

Joey's fingers held tight to the Fragment in his hand. He could feel the energy coursing through him. Beside him, Fiona balled her hands into fists that burned cobalt blue.

Elliot hopped down from the table and walked to the chair where Autumn was bound. He placed the Fragment near her face, and Joey could see fear in the girl's eyes.

One of the girls behind Elliot walked over to Joey and held her hand out, palm up. "Do the smart thing for a change," Elliot continued. "We wouldn't want anything to happen to our new friend now, would we?"

It was over. There was no way he was putting Autumn in any more danger.

Joey unwound the Fragment from his hand, removed it from the parachute cord, and laid it in the girl's waiting hand. She accepted the artifact and walked back over to Elliot.

"That's a good boy," Elliot said.

"How did you know we were here?" Rafe asked.

Elliot laughed and pointed to his shirt collar. "That scuffle you had with Tommy back in D.C.? He left you a parting gift."

Rafe reached up and ran his hand along the inside of his collar. Sure enough, he removed a miniscule, circular device. It was smaller than the pad of his index finger.

"GPS tracking instrument with full audio playback," Elliot explained. "We heard everything."

Just then, the red glow in the room wavered, and the circle of Collective goons grew fidgety.

"Joey?" Fiona sounded scared. There was a look of fright in her azure, glowing eyes. They deepened, pulsed. The energy in her hands flickered. Tendrils of blue current flowed along her dark skin, down her arms, and wrapped itself around her waist and back.

"Fiona? You okay?" Joey asked.

"I can feel them," she said. "All of them. All of their power. Joey, it's too much. I can't control it."

Energy coursed through her legs. Joey took a step toward her, and a bolt of electricity struck him in the chest, knocking him to the wooden floor.

Elliot spun to the others. "Take her out! Now!"

The Collective agents directed their Fragments at Fiona, but the artifacts began to flicker. The lightning around Fiona twisted, spun, and grew in intensity.

Blinding light exploded from around Fiona and tore through the dining room. It was followed by a deafening boom. Collective agents were tossed about like rag dolls. Joey shielded his eyes with one arm. Windows and glass cabinets shattered, and the chandelier cracked and fell. Elliot dove for cover under the table as glass and debris rained down on him.

The light vanished as swiftly as it arrived, and Fiona fell to the floor with a loud thump. Joey feared the worst until he saw her cough, and relief flooded through him. He scrambled to his feet and rushed to her side. "Fiona, are you all right?" There was a small cut on her forehead, and a trickle of blood ran down her temple and cheek. He used a sleeve to wipe it away.

Fiona looked up at him. The spark in her eyes was gone. "What's...what's going on?" she asked. Joey, I...I can't feel the Fragment anymore."

"Oh, no." There on the rug, out of arm's reach, Joey spotted a smooth, dark piece of metal.

The Fragment from Fiona's accident.

"Come on, let's go!" Rafe was cutting the rope from around Autumn and helping her to her feet. His gruff, no-nonsense voice broke through Joey's haze and spurred him to action.

Joey stood, lifting Fiona with him. She stumbled a bit, and he steadied her. "Are you okay?"

She nodded.

"What about our Fragments?" he asked Rafe.

"There's no time," Rafe barked back.

They escaped through the dining room door, leaving Elliot and the Collective stooges dazed and confused.

Once outside, Joey spied a rack of BMX bikes and skateboards leaning against the garage. "Looks like we're going to have to do this old school," he said, snatching a charcoal gray Mongoose bike with a set of back pegs on it. "Hop on and hold tight."

Fiona wrapped her arms around his chest. Beside him, Autumn grabbed one of the skateboards. Rafe was grappling with one of the Collective agents. He knocked the taser baton from the teen's hand and spun to face Joey. "What are you waiting for? Go!"

"What about you?" Joey asked.

"I'm right behind you!"

Joey furiously pedaled away from the house and the chaos they had wrought. Autumn pushed off, leaned low on the board, and followed his lead.

The driveway curved downhill, around to the front of the mansion. Joey took the turn fast, leaning left as his bike went right. Autumn did the same, crouching on her deck and gliding her right hand across the pavement.

Dang, Autumn is definitely not a noob, thought Joey.

That was good, because they didn't have time for lessons. Ahead of them, two Collective agents burst from a security building at the front of the mansion. The only way past the towering brick wall that enclosed the villa was through a wrought-iron gate.

And that gate was closing.

His calves burned as Joey pedaled faster. One of the guards aimed a tranq gun at him and fired. Joey bunny hopped into the air and twisted his handlebars in an X-up maneuver. The dart struck the bike's spokes and caromed away harmlessly. Before the teen could reload, Joey landed the move and blasted safely through the gate.

Autumn was right behind him, but the gate was closing fast. He held his breath as she expertly spun her deck until it was perpendicular to the cement and planted her feet on the wheels in a difficult move called a primo slide. Autumn balanced on the wheels as she skidded through the razor-thin gap in the closing gate. It clanged shut behind her.

Joey was impressed. "You've got skills, new girl."

"Thanks."

She pushed off down the road. Joey shook his head in amazement, then followed her toward safety.

***

Amy saw the sky outside the utility shed go supernova. Then, its accompanying shockwave rattled the walls and made the floor beneath her tremble.

"Whoa!" Peter shouted, twisting around to catch a glimpse of the light show.

It was just the opening Amy needed.

She rushed forward and drove her hands into Peter's chest. He fell back through the door, colliding with Rodney. The two toppled like bowling pins.

"Hey! Stop!" Twitch shouted, but Amy didn't listen. She escaped through the shed's door, leaping over the mass of flailing limbs.

Then she threw her Fragment into the air, where it twisted and spun until it took the shape of a sleek skateboard. She snatched the blue-tinged board in midair, dropped it to the pavement, and jumped on in one fluid motion. Thanks to the Fragment's powers, the deck's wheels glided smoothly along the asphalt.

Amy glanced behind her. Dylan was hot on her heels; the tail of his deck crackled blue as he bent low and followed her down the twisting path.

She didn't see Neelu, though.

Maybe she split off in a different direction.

The explosion from the mansion—whatever it had been—had taken its toll on the surrounding trees. The cement path was now littered with leaves and twigs. Amy swung her board expertly around them. Occasionally, she was forced to ollie or kickflip over larger, thicker branches.

Amy stole a look over her shoulder, and saw Dylan landing a 360 tre flip. The Collective goons were behind them and gaining. Dylan straightened.

Ahead, Amy saw the metal gate and brick wall that she, Dylan, and Neelu had scaled earlier. She pressed down hard on her grip tape and brought her deck to a shuddering stop.

As she kicked it up into her hand, it dissolved back into a splinter of wood.

Amy directed the Fragment at the gate, and a blast of blue energy erupted from it. The energy struck the gate, and it warped outward as if the metal bars were wet noodles. Then the gate flew open.

"Nice work!" Dylan shouted as he breezed past her.

They boarded past the broken gate, along the winding road. Dylan now took the lead, riding by moonlight and the glow of their Fragments.

There was no time to coast, though; Buzzer, Rodney, and Twitch were still nipping at their heels.

As Amy pushed herself around a bend in the road, a crimson blast struck the cement in front of her. The asphalt rippled in waves as Amy's board tried to navigate through it. She couldn't maintain control, though, and was forced to bail.

Amy hit the pavement. She rolled off the road and into the ditch, where weeds and shrubs clawed at her face and arms.

She stood and brushed herself off. Above her on the road, Buzzer stopped in front of Amy's abandoned board, watching as it shimmered, folded, and transformed into a Fragment.

Buzzer plucked the wooden artifact off the cement. It burned red in his hand. The he aimed it at Dylan— who was skating back toward Amy—and a scarlet bolt of electricity erupted from it. The shot knocked Dylan from his board.

"No!" Amy cried. She scurried up the embankment to Dylan's side. He rolled on the ground, struggling to breathe. The blast had knocked the wind from him.

"Thanks, guys," Rodney said with a sneer as he grabbed Dylan's board off the road. He rapped his knuckles against the deck's wooden tail, which now crackled red. "It's been a while since I held this bad boy."

"What do we do about them?" Twitch asked.

Peter shrugged. "We have what we need. Leave them be." For the briefest of moments, he and Amy locked eyes. She saw something in them—regret, remorse, maybe even compassion—and knew that he most likely just saved their lives.

Peter turned his back on her. "Come on, boys," he said. "Mr. Venin's gonna want to thank us."

Holding Dylan's head in her lap, Amy watched Peter, Rodney, and Twitch skate back toward the mansion and out of sight.

6

From his seated position at the desk, Archard Venin smiled and said, "The Fragments, Omar."

Omar was at a loss. If he tried to move, Tommy would tase him the same way he did Zeke. There was no way of getting out of here without playing along.

Besides, he thought, feeling the cool burn of the hawk decal tattoo on his left bicep, *I still have one trick up my sleeve. Literally.*

Omar stripped the pack off his back and removed the composite wheel bit from around his neck. He hadn't relinquished his Fragment to anyone since he'd found it at the bottom of the ocean, and it angered him to hand it over now. He slammed them both onto the oak desk. A pleased Venin reached out and seized the artifact. It danced across his long fingers.

And then the sky outside flashed white, and the house shook to its very foundation.

Dusty books toppled from the wall of shelves. The glass door leading onto the veranda shattered. Omar dove to the floor, shielding his and his father's faces as slivers of glass rained down on them.

What was that? he wondered, and then, *Man, I hope my friends are okay.*

Venin pointed at Tommy. "Find out what's going on," he insisted as the dust settled.

"Yes, sir." Tommy rushed from the room.

"You," Venin said to Omar. "Up."

Omar noticed the communication device resting loosely in Zeke's ear. *Hopefully, Neelu or Rafe still have theirs.* Unseen, he removed the earpiece, keyed it on, and slid it into his hoodie pocket. Then he stood.

Venin nodded his head at Zeke. "Lora, keep him company. If he stirs, feel free to give him another nap."

"Yes, sir." She stood over Zeke's body, taser baton at the ready.

Venin seized the backpack in one hand and grabbed Omar by the shirt with the other. He led the teen down a long hall to a bedroom guarded by two Collective agents.

Inside, a withered old man lay in bed, surrounded by a wide array of beeping machines and plastic tubes. The man did not move and, if it were not for his labored breathing, the guy would have looked dead to Omar. On a table near the bed was a pitcher of water and a plate of half-eaten food, and lying on a stack of books was—

The shield shard?!

Omar's eyes must be deceiving him. The shard from the Egyptian totem had been with Eldrick. It was lost in the San Francisco fire. How did it get here?

Venin deposited Omar's backpack on a table at the foot of the bed. He unzipped the canvas pack and removed the lead-lined box. Then they waited for the madness around them to cease.

Ten minutes passed before the door to the bedroom opened and in walked Tommy and Elliot Addison. In Elliot's hand was a small case.

"Here they are," he said. "All of our Fragments, including Rail's and the girl's."

"Fiona!" Omar's heart dropped, and his stomach twisted in a knot. *What did they do to her? The artifact was pressed against her spine, for God's sake!*

"Excellent," Venin said. He walked to an armoire and retrieved a second, larger case. "And the others?"

"Right here." Rodney's snarky voice came from the doorway. He looked sweaty and disheveled, like he'd just been running. The hulking Buzzer pushed past Rodney and into the room. His closed fist glowed an intense shade of crimson. He dropped the artifacts on the table with the others.

"How did you get those?" Omar asked. "Where are my friends?"

"Chill. Crow and Kestrel are fine, dude," Buzzer said in a low voice. Then he walked back to the door.

"Well then, let's get on with it, shall we?" Venin set the case on the table and opened it. A red light radiated out, casting his face in a crimson glow. The artifacts clattered across the table as Venin withdrew from the case the back half of a jagged skateboard. Omar saw its faded grip tape, its scuffed truck, and two polyurethane wheels with giant chunks taken out of them.

As the group watched, the loose artifacts rose into the air. Like magnets, they flew toward the larger, combined deck. As each found their place within the splintered whole, the board's red hue deepened, until it looked like a smoldering ember. Omar kept waiting for Venin to drop the board, for his hands to smoke, and for the heat to grow too hot to bear, but it never happened.

As the last remaining pieces adhered themselves to the board, Omar realized the deck was only half complete. *If this is just one half of Hawk's 900 board, then where is the rest of it?* he thought.

The final splinter of wood attached itself to the board.

And Omar's world turned upside down...

They clash. They have always clashed, two sides of the same coin. Larger than life. The black snake slithers toward him, lashes out at him with surprising speed. He flaps his wings, tries to fly, but the snake wraps itself around his legs, making flight impossible. Is it really going to end this way? Will the snake's gaping jaws and venomous fangs be the last things he will see? And then he is free, pushing off from the earth and soaring high into the clouds. There is a mountain, a city, and as he swoops back toward the ground, a massive skatepark. It is the largest he has ever seen, surrounded by a fence. Tokyo, *he thinks.* The city is Tokyo and the mountain is Mount Fuji. But why am I here? *And it hits him: this is the answer to his question. The other half of the board. The other side of the coin.*

Omar was pulled off the floor by a pair of rough hands. As his vision refocused, he saw Buzzer staring back at him.

"What's wrong with you?" Buzzer asked.

Omar shoved him away. "Nothing."

Across the room, Tommy was hauling himself to his feet as well. The two brothers locked eyes, and it was clear each was thinking the same thing: *He saw it, too.*

The rhythmic beeping from the machines quickened until it was a cacophony of sound. The elderly man on the bed sat up suddenly and gasped for breath.

"What's going on?" Rodney shouted, cupping his hands over his ears.

Venin clutched the board in front of him and let out a guttural snarl. Omar's heartbeat raced as the pieces clicked. He had seen this before, had seen the red-eyed, feverish thing Venin was transforming into in his post-apocalyptic vision.

"It's happening," he said. "The world is ending."

***

By the time Slider and Amy made it to the rendezvous point—a plaza on the southeast side of Paris—Joey, Fiona, Rafe, and the new girl, Autumn, were already there. The quartet stood beside a great stone fountain in the plaza's center. Slider was gassed; it had been a while since he'd ridden a board without a boost from his Fragment.

At least we didn't have to hoof it on foot, he thought.

After the Collective trio had left him and Amy alone and Fragment-free, the two teens had fled to the locked van, where Slider had heaved a rock through the rear window. Then he and Amy had found two spare boards under the backseat and skated into the city.

"Where are the others?" Rafe asked.

"Hey, great to see you made it out all right, too," Slider said.

"We don't know," Amy answered. "We never saw Omar or Zeke, and we lost Neelu before we'd even escaped the property."

"I don't see you sporting any blue," Joey said. He was perched on the seat of an unfamiliar BMX.

"They got our Fragments," Slider said. "You?"

"Same."

Rafe cursed under his breath.

Slider glanced around. The plaza was quite populated considering the time of night. Pedestrians, tourists with cameras, even a man walking a trio of dogs wandered past.

"How did they get the jump on us?" Slider asked.

Rafe answered. "They tagged me with an audio GPS tracker in D.C. They knew our whole plan."

"Awesome," Slider joked. "Really nice work."

"Dylan," Amy chastised him.

Rafe was the water to Slider's oil. From the minute the two had met, they'd clashed.

Rafe grabbed Slider by the shirt and lifted him off his deck. He drew back a fist, and was about to haul off, when Joey stopped him. "Hey! Chill!"

There was something odd about Rafe; his eyes were turning red, like the dude had been crying.

"Um, guys?" Autumn said from her perch on the fountain's ledge, pointing across the plaza. "You may wanna take a look at this."

What Slider saw stunned him. The man walking his dogs let go of the leashes and grabbed his head with both hands. Other pedestrians doubled over, as if in pain. On the street, a passing car swerved erratically, driving up onto the sidewalk and crashing into a cement streetlight. Nearby, a businessman in a suit unleashed a loud, low growl of anger.

"What's going on?" Amy asked, frightened. She was standing beside him now, wrapping an arm around his waist and squeezing his hand.

"George Romero zombies," Joey said. "They're turning, just like Omar said they would."

"Because the Collective has the board," Slider added. "But if all the adults are turning into zombies—"

He spun to face Rafe. The twenty-five year old's jaw was clenched tight, and his eyes had become completely bloodshot. "Run," he hissed. Then he bent in half, clawing at his neck and head.

Slider didn't hesitate. He took Amy by the arm and began to run across the plaza. "Let's go, guys! We're not safe here!" He dropped his board and jumped on.

The others followed suit. Joey helped Fiona onto the back pegs of his bike while Amy and Autumn climbed aboard their decks.

Slider had no idea where he was going. He only knew he needed to find someplace for them to hide out until Omar found them. *If* Omar found them.

Don't think like that. He's Omar. He'll be fine.

Slider carved through the plaza, weaving around a cluster of tourists who screeched and lunged at him. He twisted, turned direction, and completed a slappy 50-50 grind across a low curb to get past the group.

The adults—who by now had turned into full-fledged zombies—were quickly closing in on the Revolution teens. Slider needed to get the gang out of the plaza and onto the streets.

Ahead was a set of stairs leading down to a twisting avenue. Slider aimed for it, crouched, and leaped into the air, executing a nollie heel flip in midair. Amy and Autumn were right behind him. Amy hopped up, locked her front trucks on the stair's metal rail, and pressed her nose down in a backside overcrook. Joey shouted, "Hold tight!" as he navigated the BMX down the steps.

Slider landed hard at the bottom of the steps. His board shot out from under his feet, and he staggered backward, falling off the curb and into the street. His ankle twisted, and he hit the cement, scraping up his hands and smacking his head against the asphalt.

Slider pulled himself to his feet, brushed himself off. He hadn't spilled like that in a long time and had almost forgotten what road rash felt like.

Shouldn't try that without a helmet. I could have—

A blaring horn snapped Slider from his thoughts. He looked up as a set of headlights washed over him. A blue delivery truck careened out of control down the street, swerving back and forth.

And it was headed right toward him.

Slider's feet were rooted to the ground. He couldn't move, too frightened to act. If he didn't, though, he was going to be squished like a bug.

From nowhere, a pair of hands grabbed his shoulders. They belonged to an angry, zombified Warren Rafe. "Slider," Rafe growled. "Watch…out!"

Rafe shoved him hard out of the way of the oncoming truck. Slider reeled back; his feet hit the curb and he once more fell. As his body crumpled to the pavement, he saw the delivery truck accelerate right toward—

"Rafe!" Slider shielded his eyes as the truck passed by in a blur. He couldn't look. The truck did not stop; the zombified creature behind the wheel was either unconscious or out of control. Slider stood, wincing as he applied pressure to his twisted ankle.

Amy and the others rushed across the now-empty street. Slider was too stunned to speak.

"Come on," Amy said. "Dylan, come on."

"He…he saved my life." Slider's voice broke, and tears began to fall from his eyes.

Amy wrapped her arms around him. "Then let's make sure it stays saved," she whispered.

Slider pulled himself together, wiping his eyes with the sleeve of his hoodie. Then he crammed the Yankees cap low, snatched his lost deck off the sidewalk, and the team rode off into a city gone mad.

When Amy and Slider had escaped past Buzzer and his goons, Neelu had used the opportunity to duck back into the shed's corner, under the power breakers and out of sight. She heard the Collective teens return shortly after; she heard Rodney spouting off about stealing her friends' Fragments and asking Buzzer why they couldn't have finished them off.

Then, there was nothing but silence.

Neelu struggled to her feet. Pinpricks of pain coursed along her legs, and she tried to shake them off. Walking as quickly as she could, Neelu crossed the shed to the door. She peered out, saw no one, and exited.

Outside, she searched the underbrush for her missing earpiece. "It has to be here," she whispered, combing her fingers through the grass, dirt, and thistles. "It has to be here. It has to—bingo."

Neelu seized the earpiece out of a patch of long weeds and brought it to her ear. She heard mumbling voices. Either Zeke or Rafe had keyed his device and was letting her overhear their entire conversation.

Omar's familiar voice said, "It's happening. The world is ending."

Oh, no, Omar's been captured, and we're too late. Her mind raced. How was she going to get him out of there safely? Then it struck her, and she ran back into the utility shed.

Neelu found the largest breaker box, swung open its metal door, and found the switch labeled: Master House.

***

"Get him away from me!" Rodney shouted. A zombified Venin, still holding the 900 deck, lunged at the teen. Rodney threw up his hands to defend himself.

Omar thought of his father, who was either lying on the study floor or turning into a gnashing, snarling creature bent on attacking Lora.

How are we going to get out of this?

As if someone had heard his thoughts, the lights in the bedroom suddenly went out, shrouding them in darkness. The only illumination came from the crimson-glowing 900 deck.

Neelu, I could kiss you right now, Omar thought as he sprang into action. He rushed across the dark room to the table beside the bed, where the shield shard lay. He snatched it from atop the stack of books.

A brittle, withered hand closed around Omar's wrist. It was like being touched by death. "This is…my legacy," the old man said. His voice was a croaking whisper, as the board's possessive power took hold of him.

"Sorry," Omar answered. "It may be your legacy. But this is my world. And I plan on saving it."

He broke the man's grasp and pocketed the shard. Then he crossed to Venin and the struggling Rodney, and he quickly obtained control of the 900 deck from the unhinged Collective agent's hand. It sparked and sputtered as it exchanged owners. Omar felt its cool heat as renewed energy surged through him, and tendrils of blue and red electricity enveloped his arm.

"No!" Venin screamed, turning toward Omar.

The board, now entirely in Omar's possession, turned a vibrant blue. He broke for the door, saw Buzzer lunging at him, and skidded to a stop. The teen missed him by an inch, slamming instead into the wall.

Omar escaped into the open hall. He threw the board in front of him.

The board shimmered and transformed into a whole deck, and he leaped on. Guided only by the light emanating around him from his skateboard, he glided across the wooden floor, rocketing toward the study.

When Omar burst into the room, Zeke was awake and standing. There was a look of confusion in his eyes. Lora cowered in the corner. Her taser had been cast aside. "Stay away from him," Lora warned. "Something's…wrong."

"It's all right now," Omar told her.

"What happened to me?" Zeke asked. The effects of the board were wearing off.

"I'll explain later. We have to go." Omar pulled his father through the shattered glass door. They crossed the veranda, and without thinking, Omar jumped onto the stone railing and leaped off. He hit the grass, and Zeke landed beside him a second later.

They took off across the lawn, toward the back driveway and the safety of the trees. Omar craned his neck to look back and saw the yard swarming with Collective agents—and Venin. A tranq dart sliced through the air to his left. Omar ran faster. Another dart narrowly missed his sweatshirt's hood. A third missed Zeke's leg by a millimeter.

As they passed the guest house and utility shed, Omar heard a voice cry out, "Omar! Zeke! Wait for me!"

Neelu burst from of the utility shed with her head low. She sprinted across the lawn toward Omar, and he slowed down a bit, giving her a chance to catch up. As he reached out to take her hand, though, a tranq dart struck her in the small of the back.

"Neelu!" Omar shouted. She staggered forward, right into his waiting arms.

The Collective teens were closing in. They were going to be captured again. And there was nothing Omar could do about it.

The pocket of his hoodie suddenly burned as if it were on fire, and a drumming sensation filled his head and heart. The answer was there, waiting for him.

He needed a shield.

Omar dug into his pocket and removed the wooden shield shard. It glowed white-hot. Omar held the shard in front of him with one hand as Zeke scooped the unconscious Neelu from his other.

An explosion erupted from the shard, radiating outward. A shimmering force field encircled Omar, Zeke, and Neelu, like an enormous bubble. The Collective teens were forced to stop in their tracks.

Rodney pressed to the front of the gang lining the force field. He grabbed his skateboard by the tail and swung it fiercely. As it struck the energy field, the deck disintegrated until it was nothing but a couple of sizzling metal trucks.

"Catch ya later, gang," Omar said.

Then, still holding the shard out to protect them, Omar and Zeke ran with an immobilized Neelu into the woods, back toward the van.

***

"Man, this place is giving me the creeps." Amy's sentiment echoed throughout the underground chamber. They were deep below the streets of Paris, making their way through a maze of tunnels known as the Catacombs.

"We had to get off the streets," Joey said from his position at the front of the group. "Who knows how long that craziness will last?"

"And this place is safe?" Amy asked.

"Let's hope so."

They pressed on. It was cool and dark down in the cave. Joey ran his hand along one of the stone walls, then swept his flashlight across the chamber ahead. He was met by the hollow stares of a thousand skulls.

"What is this place?!" shouted Fiona. "A cemetery?"

"Yep," Autumn answered. "They're actually stone mines that were renovated into a mass burial site a couple hundred years ago. Now it's a tourist attraction."

Joey turned and looked back at the red-haired teen.

Autumn shrugged. "What? I had a history test last week. Which I aced, by the way."

Joey just shook his head and continued walking. The chamber opened up into a small space with a few support pillars and a stone lamp on a pedestal. The wall of skulls continued; they were crammed into every spare inch of space.

The group paused here to catch their breath.

"Everyone okay?" Joey asked.

They all nodded—everyone except Slider, who leaned against one of the pillars, lost in thought. Joey was worried about his friend. He hadn't spoken a word since they'd fled the plaza, and when they'd needed to break the lock to gain entrance to the catacombs, Slider had violently bashed it open with the tail of his skateboard. It had splintered the board nearly in two and left Slider with bloodied fingers.

"Dude, you can't fall apart on us, okay?" Joey told Slider. "I need your help."

For a moment, Slider did not respond. Then he said, "He just...I mean, he...sacrificed himself. For me."

"Yeah. It was a brave thing to do."

"But...I thought he hated me."

"We're a team," Amy said from behind Joey. She took Slider's hand in hers. Then she took Joey's. "We're a team, and we look out for one another. Despite your differences, Rafe knew that, Dylan."

They stood that way for a moment, three of the four original members of the Revolution.

"She's right," Joey said. "And if the world ends tonight, we're going out together." He nodded to Fiona and Autumn, and the two girls joined them. Fiona wrapped her arms around Joey's waist, immediately putting him at ease.

"We're not a whole team yet, though," Slider said.

"The others are safe," Amy said. "They have to be. And they'll come back to us."

"I hope you're right," Fiona said.

Me too, Joey thought. *Because hope is all we have left.*

***

"This is all the Collective's fault." Omar leaned forward and peered out the van's windshield at the street in front of them.

A number of cars sat either in the middle of the road or had crashed up onto the sidewalk. A small fire burned from the hood of one. A few of the cars' drivers stood outside their vehicles, speaking to one another or standing in awe on the sidewalk.

Zeke navigated around the stalled and crushed vehicles, turned left onto a side street free of cars, and continued toward the rendezvous point.

Neelu stirred, and Omar twisted in his seat to look back at where she lay sprawled out on the backseat.

"How do you feel?" he asked.

"Like I've been tumbling around in an undertow." She sat up, then clutched her head and winced.

"Just take it easy. And thanks for the save out there."

"Any time."

"Here we are," Zeke said, stopping the van near a set of stairs. He threw the vehicle in park and hopped out.

"If you don't mind, I think I'm just gonna chill out here," Neelu said, sliding back down in her seats.

Together, Zeke and Omar bounded up the steps and into the plaza. Omar searched for the others, spying a man trying to calm three leashed dogs and a young couple hugging one another beside a large fountain.

But no Revolution.

"This is the rendezvous point, right?" Omar asked, though he knew the answer.

"They must have fled when the insanity started," Zeke surmised. "Found someplace safe to hide out."

"Let's hope so." Omar fished around in his hoodie, pulling out his smartphone and keying in Joey's cell number. He held his breath as it rang.

Then, "O! You're all right!"

Omar had never been so excited to hear Joey's voice before. The feeling seemed mutual. "Where are you guys?" he asked.

"In the Land of the Heebie-Jeebies," Joey said without a shred of humor.

***

Twenty minutes later, the entire team was back in the van, heading toward Charles De Gaulle Airport again, where Sam was waiting with the chopper. Traffic wasn't terrible; the damage varied throughout the city, with the tourist places getting hit hardest. Zeke stuck to side roads, and they only had to stop once, when two police cars had blocked an intersection because one car had T-boned another.

Omar couldn't believe that Rafe was gone. Amy's recounting of the incident brought him to tears.

This really was the end. Whatever games they'd been playing, whatever exotic locales they'd visited and near-death experiences they'd had, it was nothing compared to the last few days.

One bright spot in the madness, though, was Fiona. Omar recalled Elliot Addison bringing the twisted piece of metal that had been wedged near her spine to Venin, and he had feared she was mortally wounded. But here she was. Safe. And, aside from a gap in her memory surrounding the explosion she'd caused at the mansion, she was unharmed.

When Omar was done explaining what had happened to Zeke, Neelu, and himself, Joey asked, "So wait. We only have half the board?"

Omar held up the Birdman's 900 deck, showing off the splintered edges where the remainder of the board would fit. "Yeah. The Collective still has the other half."

"In Tokyo?" Autumn asked.

Omar nodded.

"Then let's go find it and end this once and for all," Slider said with finality. Omar couldn't agree more. It was now or never.

8

It was a long flight to Tokyo, twelve hours at least, and they left Paris as the beginnings of daylight tinged the horizon. Zeke ordered the team to rest—they were going on little to no sleep as it was—and this time, Omar found he could relax. It was probably because of the calming effects of the glowing board at his feet. But hey, he wasn't going to look a gift horse in the mouth.

He did not dream, and when his eyes fluttered open and he swam up from the depths of deep sleep, he saw from his window the majestic peak of Mount Fuji, Japan's highest mountain, in the distance.

His dad sat across from him, eating an energy bar and reading his electronic notepad. "Good morning," he said, tossing a wrapped bar at Omar. "Looks like you needed some sleep."

"I guess." Omar toed the board at his feet. *Still there.*

"We're close. I know we made good time, but we need to be prepared. The Collective to already be here waiting for us. Especially if Tommy saw the same imagery as you in the vision you told me about."

Omar tore open an energy bar and took a bite. "He did. I know he did."

"Holy…" Joey said from the other side of the chopper. "I'm going to guess that's it."

Omar leaned over to look out Joey's window. The others did the same. Below them lay a sprawling complex surrounded by a tall, chain-link fence. It was the largest outdoor skatepark Omar had ever seen, with a series of clover-shaped bowls, massive vert ramps splashed with brightly colored graffiti, and a street section with an insane amount of ledges.

Sam brought the helicopter down on a patch of blacktop near the park's entrance, and Zeke threw open the side door. Omar was immediately beset by swirling wind. He clutched his portion of the 900 deck under his arm, lowered his head, and jumped from the Blackhawk.

When the team was safely on ground—all but Autumn, who stayed in the chopper with Sam—the Blackhawk lifted into the cloudless sky.

Before them was a large, chain-link gate. Through it, Omar saw the course inside, with soaring ramps and pipes. He held the board high and stepped in front of the others.

For a long time, nothing happened. Then a person appeared, walking through the complex and stopping at the gate. Archard Venin.

"Good afternoon, old friend," Venin said. "I see you've wasted no time getting here."

"Says the man who greets us," Zeke answered.

Venin's smile was filled with malice. "Then let us get down to business. I propose an offer."

"What's that?"

"A challenge of skills. Your son versus my protégé, Tommy Goff. The winner receives the 900 skateboard in its entirety."

"What?!" Slider yelled. "You've got to be kidding me."

But he wasn't, and Omar knew it. He thought it over. They could storm the Collective's complex, try their best to secure the board. But who else would be hurt in the process? Slider? Amy?

Neelu?

No. It was too risky.

The choice was simple. It was another vision coming true. The bird and the serpent, forever clashing.

He turned to the others. "I'll be fine," he said. "I can do this."

"Then we'll be right here, O," Joey said. "Just waiting to get your back." He held out a hand, and Omar slapped him five.

He took a deep breath and exhaled slowly. Then he turned to face Venin and shouted, "Okay! We agree!"

Zeke placed a hand on Omar's shoulder. "Are you sure about this, son?"

"Absolutely," was his answer.

"Then let's go win this thing."

With one last look back at his friends, and with his father trailing behind him, Omar stepped across the threshold, into the lion's den.

***

Omar and Zeke followed Venin through the course, walking around at least a half dozen clover bowls with steel coping. A few had cradle bowls jutting out of them, and in the middle of one was a mound known as a twinkie. A nearby kidney-shaped pool had a wall on one side. A splat wall. *Sick*. Just thinking about skating in such a place was making Omar's stomach twist.

"What up, bro?" Tommy's voice echoed across the course. It took Omar a second to find him, standing atop the first in a line of half-pipes. *That has to be at least a twenty-foot transition,* Omar thought.

On each side of the vert ramp was a ladder inset in the frame. Venin tossed a helmet at Omar, then climbed up to join Tommy on the ramp's deck. Omar clamored up the other side. Zeke followed him to the top.

They faced off, Revolution against Collective, good versus evil. There was roughly two hundred feet of pipe between them, and the battle began.

Omar
VERSUS
Tommy

HUH?!

"You can't outskate me," said Tommy after their brief battle. "I taught you everything you know."

"Not everything. I've got a few surprise moves."

"Ah, like that fancy tattoo of yours? Yeah, I got myself one of those, too."

Tommy pulled back his T-shirt sleeve. There on his shoulder was a circular decal: black, white, and red. A single word—*FURY*—was written in white. It was the name of one of Tony Hawk's sponsors.

The decal moved along Tommy's arm. He clutched it in his hand and then slid it into Venin's waiting palm. Venin threw his head back. Omar watched, amazed, as the man's neck elongated. Veins of black and blue contorted around him, enveloped him.

Holy…he's turning into a giant snake.

Sure enough, when the change was complete, Venin had become a sleek, black serpent. The snake protected Tommy by curling around the boy's legs and feet.

Omar's hawk decal burned against his bicep, itching to be free. Zeke understood what had to be done. He grabbed Omar's forearm and let the decal transfer from son to father.

In the same way Venin had metamorphosed, Zeke's arms grew long at his sides. He sprouted brown feathers, flapping his wings and rising into the air until he hovered over Omar's shoulder as a mighty hawk.

"Let's see what you've got!" Tommy called. In his hands now was the other half of the mystical skateboard. It gleamed a deep crimson, then shimmered and became whole.

Omar did the same. He could feel the power of the 900 deck rushing through him. It quickened his pulse, calmed his nerves.

Without pause, Omar dropped over the steel coping into the ramp. Tommy gave a hoot of delight, then followed suit.

They rocketed down their respective transitions, hurtling toward one another under the power of the Birdman's mystical board.

***

Ominous clouds filled the sky, swirling around the skatepark and casting it in shadow. They reminded Joey of images from a hurricane. *And we're smack dab in the eye of the storm.*

He climbed the chain-link fence, hoping to get a better view inside the park.

"What do you see?" Amy asked.

On the street outside the fenced-in skatepark, two grown-ups were slowly ambling toward them. Even from here, Joey could see their blood-shot eyes and foaming mouths. "Zombies."

"It's happening again," Fiona said. "Just like Paris."

The zombies were like cockroaches crawling out in the darkness. Joey had lost count; if not for the towering chain-link fence, the complex would already have been overrun. To his left, a mass of fifty zombies clawed at one another and pressed against the fence. The metal was beginning to bend; if it broke, they'd be goners, for sure.

Thankfully, Omar had prepared for this possibility. Joey keyed the sleek earpiece he was wearing. "Sam!" he shouted. "Tell Autumn to do it!"

"Copy that," came the pilot's response.

Joey stepped back, waving at the others. "Push in," he said. "Get as close to the park as you can."

***

Autumn sat in the Blackhawk, clutching the shield shard to her chest. In less than 48 hours, she had gone from being a normal teenage girl who panicked when she was late to cheerleading practice to part of a team whose mission was to save the world.

The pilot, Sam, spoke into his headset. Then he swiveled in his seat and said, "You're up."

Autumn nodded and moved to the large side door of the chopper. A thick canvas harness was strung around her waist. She grabbed one of its trailing cords and attached it to a bar above the Blackhawk's door. She wasn't nervous; the exhilaration of what she was about to do was overwhelming.

I'm saving the world. How crazy is that?

Autumn yanked the door open. Lashing wind whipped her red hair around her face. She looked out and saw the skatepark far below her—and what looked like an enormous hawk wrestling with a snake in midair. Her heart pounded in her chest like a timpani.

She stepped out onto the chopper's skid, thanking her lucky stars for the harness.

"Here goes nothing." Autumn held the shard at arm's lengths. It suddenly went from being an ancient hunk of scrap to a pulsing white artifact.

A streak of electricity burst from the shard, and a field of energy stretched out and encapsulated the whole skatepark in one massive force field.

***

There had to have been over a thousand zombies now, each and every one of them pressing against the fence. It angled down, only a few seconds away from giving in entirely.

The glimmering energy field struck the ground less than fifty feet from the Revolution teens. Even though he knew it was coming, Joey leaped back as the barrier rippled the cement in front of them.

The zombies screamed in protest, but they must have sensed the force field's dangerous power; it stopped them in their tracks.

Joey breathed a temporary sigh of relief.

Okay. Now let's just hope Omar ends this quickly.

***

Omar and Tommy had gone from shredding the vert ramps to navigating the field of pools. They moved fast, whipping past one another at blazing speeds.

Tommy soared from one pool to another by doing a backside air. Omar arced around a full-pipe capsule, sending bolts of electricity in every direction. At one point, Omar performed a 360 as Tommy soared over his head in a tuck-knee backflip.

Omar sensed that he and Tommy could keep up this display of skill for hours. It was amazing, really. How far they'd come from being just a couple of posers in SoCal who watched crappy VHS tapes of the X-Games in his bedroom. Or from skating the Imperial Beach Pier and taping their moves in hopes of landing a sponsor.

That's it, Omar thought. *I know how to get under Tommy's skin.*

As Tommy curved expertly up and down a cradle bowl, Omar shouted, "Yo, Tommy! Your dad says hi!"

"Liar!" Tommy shouted back.

"It's true! He's working for the Revolution."

This comment hit Tommy like a cannonball to the chest. He wavered on his deck and tried to regain control but was forced to bail. He pinwheeled through the air and landed on his back at the bottom of a pool.

Omar changed directions and steered to where Tommy lay.

A hissing erupted from the sky, and Omar looked up to see the snake trying desperately to tear itself free from the hawk. It lunged down at Omar, opening its venomous fangs. They snapped shut just above his head.

Tommy groaned as Omar reached the top of the pool. Looking down, Omar asked, "You okay?"

Tommy ignored him. He stood and snatched up his board.

"Your dad is safe, Tommy," Omar said. "He asked me to bring you home safe to him."

"Stop lying to me," Tommy said. His voice broke a little; Omar was getting to him.

"It's Venin who's been lying. About your dad. About your destiny. We don't know our destinies, Tommy. Can't you see that?"

"I heard them. I heard Eldrick and your dad. They wanted to get rid of me, Omar. Throw me away like a piece of trash."

Omar shook his head. "Lies."

Above them, the snake hissed again.

"Tommy, a while ago, you wanted me to join you, to be a family again. I can do this; I can complete the 900 board and make sure its power is used for the right reasons. But I can't do it alone."

Omar slid down the embankment, into the empty pool to stand beside Tommy. His board changed back into its original shape. He held out his hand to Tommy.

"What do you say, bro?" Omar asked.

"And my dad?"

"He misses you." There was a pause. Then, Omar added, "I miss you."

Tommy looked up at the writhing, hissing serpent. "But I've...I've done some terrible things, O."

"They can be forgiven. Because that's what family does. They forgive one another."

The snake struggled again, tried to dive down at the two boys.

Tommy stared it down. Then he turned and shook Omar's hand. "Yeah. I'm in."

His board, which had been flickered a dull red, was washed of color. It transformed into the mirror image of Omar's deck.

The two teens stood facing one another.

Then, together, they reattached the two halves of Tony Hawk's 900 skateboard.

The sky erupted in thunder. The ground shook, and the cement pool they stood in cracked and crumbled.

"Noooo!" the serpent screeched.

The hawk dove toward the ground. The two creatures distorted and changed until they were human again. The decals sprang forth from their skin, latching on to the deck as it trembled in Omar's hands. The most brilliant blue light Omar had ever seen burst from the skateboard, rising into the air, shattering the force field surrounding the skatepark. The light took the shape of a hawk whose wingspan stretched miles across the sky.

Omar was lifted off his feet. He fought hard to control the board, to harness its energy. He felt a trickle of blood escape his nose, felt Tommy's arms wrap around his waist, and then—

He sees the world, in flashes and all of it at once. It is not free of war, of disease, of death or heartbreak, but it has the potential to be. This new world that the Revolution has helped create is a world of hope. Of life that can be lived without fear. He feels it in his heart and knows that every soul in the world has the potential to feel it as well. He has done it. No, they have done it. As a team.

Omar opened his eyes. The sun was breaking through the gray clouds and casting its light down on them. High above, a flock of birds—a rail, a crow, a kestrel, a skylark, an otus, and of course, a brown and black grebe—flew together. Omar smiled.

***

"Omar. Omar." Her voice came to him softly, as if he was hearing her from a great distance or from the depths of an ocean. It was a fitting thought; after all, she had on several occasions saved him from drowning.

His eyes fluttered open, and there she was: Neelu, staring down at him. Her caramel-colored dreads dangled like wind chimes around her face. She smiled.

"Hi," he croaked. His mouth felt like someone had poured the Sahara Desert into it.

Omar scanned his surroundings. He was in a hospital room of sorts. White walls and no windows.

Neelu noticed his curiosity. "We're at the Wyvern. You've been out of it for a while."

"How long?"

"A couple of days."

Days?! Omar sat up in bed. He shouldn't be sore, no more than usual, yet it took a great deal of effort to lift his head off the pillow.

Neelu reached for an electronic tablet on a nearby table, pressing a series of buttons. Then she spoke into it. "Guys. He's awake."

Omar ran a hand through his hair. "So have you been here the whole time?"

"Don't flatter yourself. We've taken turns." She placed a hand over his. "I've taken a few more turns than the others, though."

She told him what happened, to the best of her knowledge. After the board had been completed, the spell cast on the citizens of Tokyo had broken. They'd been lost, confused, but mostly unharmed. "The media is blaming the craziness on a gas leak," she added. "Though the U.S. government has spent a pretty penny getting their hands on all of the video footage of some ridiculous blue hawk in the sky."

There was a knock on the door. Joey, Fiona, Amy, and Slider stood waiting to enter. Neelu leaned in and kissed him softly on the lips. "I'll be back later." His pulse quickened like he was holding a Fragment again. Neelu slid out past the others.

"Wow," Joey mouthed as they entered. He winked at Omar, as if to say, "Nicely done, sir."

Omar was happy to see them and to know that they were all safe. They talked for a long while, regaling one another with stories about the final confrontation. Joey told him how Zeke had led Archard Venin out of the compound in handcuffs, while Slider was envious of Omar for shredding on the massive vert ramps.

"Where's Autumn?" Omar asked.

"She flew back to D.C. yesterday," Amy told him.

"And I'm on my way back to San Diego later today," Fiona announced. "The doctors here gave me a clean bill of health."

Omar glanced at Joey. He didn't seem entirely thrilled about Fiona leaving.

"What about you?" Omar asked Slider and Amy.

"Well, I'm going to try my luck in Colorado," Slider announced. "I figure I should see something other than buildings, maybe hone my snowboarding skills." He tapped his hat. "Don't get any ideas, though. You can take the kid out of New York, but you can't convince him to be anything but a Yankees fan."

They all shared a good laugh. Then the quartet prepared to leave.

"Get some rest," Amy said.

"Okay." Omar closed his eyes but found that he was too worked up to sleep any more. So he poured himself a glass of water, flipped on a small flat-screen television stationed on the far wall, and caught the end of a news story about all of the wild conspiracies surrounding the peculiar incident in Japan.

"Knock, knock."

Tommy now stood at the door, a remorseful look in his eyes. He entered, quickly followed by Henry and Zeke.

"How are you feeling?" his father asked.

"All right," Omar answered, taking a long drink of water.

Henry came over to the bed and held out his hand to shake. Omar accepted. "Thank you," Henry said. "Thank you for helping me get my family back."

"Hey, we're all family," Omar said, looking at Tommy. "Right?"

Tommy nodded. "Right."

Zeke answered the remainder of Omar's questions about the Collective —"The authorities are rounding up and rooting out each and every one of them"—about the old man—"He was Venin's father and is resting comfortably in a hospital in Washington"—and about the location of the 900 board and the shield shard— "Classified."

Tommy and Henry announced that they were leaving for home, once the Wyvern was officially decommissioned, and taking a very long vacation as a family. "We've got a lot of catching up to do," Henry said, draping his arm over his son's shoulder.

Tommy and Omar exchanged the elaborate handshake they'd developed as kids, and it was alarming to Omar that he remembered it so well. "Some things never change," he said.

"And some change for the better," said Tommy.

***

A week later, at Arlington National Cemetery, a service was held for both Eldrick Otus and Warren Rafe. The entire Revolution—Autumn included—was in attendance. Omar held Neelu's hand through the entire thing, stood by her side as men and women who'd served in the military with Eldrick came to offer their condolences, to shake her hand, and in some cases, to share a hug or a fond memory.

After, while Neelu hung back with Zeke to sign some paperwork, the others changed clothes at their hotel and walked to a nearby skatepark that Autumn frequented. A number of kids were either grinding ledges or skating its modest half-pipes.

Finally, they took a break, sprawling out in the grass beneath a tall oak tree. Autumn and Fiona offered to buy refreshments at a concession stand. "I can work my magic on Seth, the dude behind the stand," Autumn said with a smile.

That left the original four members of the Revolution. They sat quietly together for some time before Joey spoke.

"It seems crazy," he said. "After all we've done, nobody evens realizes that things are different."

"Maybe that's the point," Amy said. "If everyone knew they'd been given a gift, how many people would have squandered it? Let it pass them by?"

"Look at the Birdman, for example," Slider said. "He spent years and years practicing his sport. He worked hard, persevered, and was rewarded for it."

Omar agreed. "I think that whatever gave the 900 board its power, it started with Tony Hawk for a reason. Because he exemplifies the potential for greatness that we all have, if we choose to earn it."

Omar looked out across the skatepark and spied a couple of kids, no older than seven, who were tentatively stepping onto their boards. They were noobs for sure, and the sight of them made Omar smile.

Because of the Revolution, they had the power to be anything they dreamed they could be.

THE END

ABOUT TONY HAWK

TONY HAWK is the most famous and influential skateboarder of all time. In the 1980s and 1990s, he was instrumental in skateboarding's transformation from fringe pursuit to respected sport. After retiring from competitions in 2000, Tony continues to skate demos and tour all over the world.

He is the founder, president, and CEO of Tony Hawk, Inc., which he continues to develop and grow. He is also the founder of the Tony Hawk Foundation, which works to create skateparks and empower youth in low-income communities.

ABOUT THE AUTHOR_

BRANDON TERRELL is a Saint Paul-based writer and filmmaker. He has worked on television commercials and independent feature films for almost a decade. He has also written dozens of comic books and children's books. When not writing, Brandon enjoys watching movies, reading, baseball, and spending time with his wife Jen and their son Alex.

AUTHOR Q & A_

Q: WHEN DID YOU DECIDE TO BECOME A WRITER?

A: I've been writing and telling stories all of my life. I still have notebooks filled with childhood mysteries I wrote that were inspired by The Hardy Boys and Encyclopedia Brown. I love the idea of engaging a reader by finding an unexpected way to tell a story. It's been a lifelong passion of mine.

Q: DESCRIBE YOUR APPROACH TO THE TONY HAWK'S 900 REVOLUTION SERIES.

A: My approach always starts with the characters and trying to find new and exciting ways for them to showcase their extreme talents, while still telling a story that packs an emotional punch. Then I try to imagine locations that are visually interesting as well, places where the Revolution team will be out of their element. While I'm not a globe-trotting traveler myself, some of the locations I've written about are places I've visited at one time or another. What's fascinating about the series is that it blends multiple genres (mystery, action, science fiction, romance, etc.) all in one book, so the story possibilities are endless!

TONY HAWK'S 900 revolution

VOL. 1: DROP IN

VOL. 2: IMPULSE

VOL. 3: FALL LINE

VOL. 7: EXILED

VOL. 8: LOCKDOWN

VOL. 9: ZOMBIFIED

VOL. 10: UNEARTHED

VOL. 11: FLIPSIDE

VOL. 12: RECHARGED

VOL. 13: HORIZON

COLLECT THE FULL SERIES!